For Dara

Published in 1993 by
Stewart, Tabori & Chang
575 Broadway, New York, New York 10012

Library of Congress Cataloging-in-Publication Data
O'Malley, Kevin, 1961–
The box / Kevin O'Malley.
p.   cm.
Summary: A boy and his teddy bear share some adventures when they
take a trip to another planet in a cardboard box.
ISBN 1-55670-275-2
[1. Play—Fiction.   2. Teddy bears—Fiction.   3. Stories without
words.]   I. Title.
PZ7.0526Bo   1993
[E]—dc20   92-25153
CIP

Distributed in the U.S. by
Workman Publishing, 708 Broadway
New York, New York 10003

Distributed in Canada by
Canadian Manda Group, P.O. Box 920 Station U
Toronto, Ontario M8Z 5P9

Distributed in all other territories (except Central and South America) by
Melia Publishing Services, P.O. Box 1639
Maidenhead, Berkshire, SL6 6YZ England

Central and South American accounts should contact
Export Sales Manager, Stewart, Tabori & Chang

Printed in Italy
10 9 8 7 6 5 4 3 2 1

THE BOX

Kevin O'Malley

Stewart, Tabori & Chang
New York